COLD LAKE ANTHOLOGY 2021

Cold Lake Anthology 2021

SELECTIONS FROM THE BURLINGTON WRITERS
WORKSHOP

*Editors Elaine Pentaleri and Nancy
Volkers; Intern Taylor Rossics*

Cold Lake Publishing

CONTENTS

~ ~

A NOTE FROM THE EDITORS

All water has a perfect memory and is forever trying to get back to where it was.

Toni Morrison

We invite you into the waters of memory, reflection, and reverie fathomed by the writers in this 2021 issue of Cold Lake Anthology.

From our opening story—*Ice,* by Mary Chafee, in which the main character undulates between dream and reality and comes to face his own death—to the philosophical and poetic musings of Jonah Meyer's closing piece *Form 4-B, to be attached to application materials, in consideration of employment,* the stories and poems in this collection pull time from its depths, grasp it by the tendrils, and invite us to understand.

The beneficial aquatic plant *Chara* can be planted by simply throwing it in the water, where it will grow when it receives sunlight. Our memories, reflections and reveries are like that: they grow where we provide them with light. Archaeology, historical recounting, family history, love's yearnings, and nostalgia for the accoutrements of the past are realized here.

We hope you enjoy this anthology. As you find yourself submerged in memory, reflection, and reverie, may there be sunlight to guide you through.

Elaine Pentaleri

Nancy Volkers

ICE - MARY D. CHAFFEE

When the ice storm struck he'd been dreaming of his dead wife, her pleasant, creased face turned away, talking to someone he couldn't see. He woke in the darkest part of the night to the sound of the wind rising in the tall pines beside the driveway, to Bella whining nervously in her basket.

Sleet hissed down, then hail rattled like sharp little claws on the deck's warped floorboards. The old house creaked. Downstairs a door rattled in concert with the wind's gusts. The wind was stronger in the pines now, starting low and building to a roar.

Bella jumped onto the bed, seeking comfort. Pushing the little dog aside, he fumbled for the bedside lamp's light switch, but when he flicked it back and forth nothing happened. Favoring his knee, he hoisted himself carefully to his feet and thought about where a flashlight might be.

The house shook as the nor'easter gathered strength. The breaker box seemed a long way off. After a moment he clambered clumsily back into bed, pulled the old down comforter around him, and managed to fall back to sleep.

Thanks to god or the electric company, the power was back on in the morning, He fed Bella and shooed the reluctant animal out the back door into a world sheathed in ice. It glittered with malevolent beauty, forcing every twig and branch to bow to its authority.

Bella scratched at the door and he let her back inside. He fixed himself a breakfast his doctor wouldn't have approved of and took a cup of instant coffee to the front room, leaving the greasy frying pan and dirty dishes to clean themselves.

The sun had already been and gone. New snow clouds were moving in, turning the sky a thick, darkening gray. Peering through the smudged glass of the sitting room's bay window he spotted what might have been the white mail delivery truck, almost invisible against the streetscape's bleached background.

He felt a small thrill of anticipation. The mailman's – no, the *mail delivery person*'s – regular visit had become the high point of his day. No matter that the mail usually consisted of advertising for items he didn't want, credit card offers to 'current resident' or begging letters for causes his softhearted wife had supported.

All trash. But the carrier...ah, that was a difference matter entirely. Last spring he'd been grubbing on his knees in the leaf-matted flowerbed by the mailbox at the end of the long driveway when a shadow fell on him. He looked around, dazzled by the westering sun. Dazzled, then, by the uniformed vision in blue with a heavy mailbag by her side, a rangy high-breasted girl with a mass of thick white-gold hair spilling out from under the regulation blue cap that matched her eyes perfectly.

She held out a motley collection of circulars, form letters, the usual crap.

"Dyer, number 36? Your mail." A sweet voice, with laughter in it.

"Where's Jack," he blurted, then bit his lip, but she didn't seem offended.

"Jack's retired," she said. "He's probably fishing as we speak. I'm Jenny, his replacement."

That's how it had begun. He'd watch for her truck and manage to be walking down the driveway just as she was about to put his mail in the box -- a patent ruse recognized but unacknowledged by both parties. He'd call hello, she'd give him his mail and they'd chat for a few moments.

He couldn't see worth a damn through the window. So he limped over to where his parka was lying on the floor, shrugged it on and squinted out toward the street from the stoop outside the mud porch. His eyes were watering from the bitter cold, but through the tears he could make out a female shape with a bag at the far end of the long driveway.

Jenny, right on time despite the storm.

Hobbling slightly, he went down the steps to meet her. The shape drew closer. Its hair was old-lady white, not white gold. He pulled back but it was too late. She'd seen him.

"Helloo, Mister Dyer!"

KItty Flowers, damn it all to hell. He stood watching her as she shuffled determinedly up the ice-clad driveway.

"Kitty, what in the world were you thinking?"

She'd made it to the bottom of the steps and was still catching her breath, a generous-sized woman slipping comfortably into middle age. At his question her wide mouth twisted into an expression of mock disapproval.

"Good morning to you, too, Allen."

"No, what I meant to say was..." He frowned at the ice-shrouded landscape. "Aren't you afraid of breaking something?"

"Me? Nah. I got my micro-spikes on. And if I fall, I just bounce."

Guess your fat makes a good airbag he thought, but didn't say.

"Wicked bad last night, right?" said Kitty. "Lost my electric. But luckily it was on again this morning." She rummaged in her bag and brought out a foil wrapped throwaway pan. "I baked you a coffee cake. Apricots and maple syrup."

"I'm allergic to apricots," he said, though he wasn't.

"You can pick 'em out," said Kitty, cheerfully oblivious to his rude behavior. "I've been worrying about you, Allen. I'll just bet you don't eat right since Dolores passed," she said. "Here ya go."

He took the pan from her outstretched hands, muttering a thank you. *Damn woman.* He'd tolerated her as a friend of his wife's. But Dolores was barely cold in her coffin when Kitty had begun dropping by, inviting him to dinner, offering to take Bella for a walk. She'd lost her husband to a heart attack several years ago. Was she prospecting for another one? If so, she'd find only old fool's gold at his place.

"I won't stay," Kitty said, though he hadn't invited her in. "Just wanted to check on you after that doozy of a storm. You take good care of that leg now. When you get to be 'our' age..." she said, though he had at least fifteen years on her, and smiled to take the sting out of it. As she trudged away snowflakes drifted from the louring sky.

The biting cold seemed to have followed him inside. To warm himself up he fixed a pot of tea, poured a dollop of whiskey into it and tried several times to get a fire going in the front room's old Hearthstone wood stove. When he finally got it started, the fire burned low and smoky, more trouble than it was worth.

He sat in the silent room, one eye on the driveway, brooding. How had that damned woman known about his injury? And wasn't it just like her to assume it was his leg that was hurting instead of getting her facts straight. It was his knee, dammit. His *knee.* When the doctor had diagnosed his painfully swollen knee as gout, he'd laughed cynically. "Gout? The rich man's disease?" But the doctor, her face serious, had referred him to Rheumatology, where he'd been given prescriptions for unpronounceable medicines, and told to lay off the booze.

The distant rumble of the approaching snow plough barely penetrated the silence of the living room. He poured another splash of whiskey into his mug of tea, and cut himself a healthy slice of Kitty's coffee cake to go with it.

Cake for his lunch, with nobody to give him grief about it.

The sky was darkening. He checked his watch. Later than he thought, almost half-past three. Very late for the mail. Had he somehow missed the arrival of Jenny's truck? No, not possible. He'd been in the living room all afternoon, watching out for it. The bad weather had delayed the truck, he thought, that must be it.

It had been snowing lightly earlier in the day, but when he went to put Bella out again the snow had given way to what the weather lady called a wintry mix. Freezing rain, sleet, snow – a little of everything nasty. It was pelting down harder now. Bella cowered by his legs, skinny tail down, until he pushed her outside and slammed the door. Bella was an elderly rescue from the Humane Society – part Chihuahua, part Shih Tzu and as far as he was concerned, one hundred percent wimp. She'd been Dolores's baby. But Dolores was gone, leaving the little dog on his hands.

When he finally remembered to let Bella back in she was shivering, and ice was crusted on the pads of her paws. She followed him back to the living room and curled up near the woodstove's meager warmth, licking at her paws. He settled on the couch with a novel, a beer and a bag of potato chips, but the story wasn't very interesting and he soon threw it aside. Then the beer began to take effect and he closed his eyes, just for a minute...

He dreamed again of his dead wife, Dolores. She was standing at the foot of his bed. Her lips were moving but he couldn't hear her voice. Her lined face wore an anxious expression. She was trying to tell him something important.

Her hair was the soft auburn of her youth; he'd loved to stroke it, once.

He woke on the couch with a foul taste in his mouth and a full bladder. The fire had gone out and it was very cold. It was in the bathroom, when he had cleared the sleep from his eyes, that he noticed something strange. A delicate scurf of gray ice had formed around the windowsill, and where the tiled floor met the baseboard; it looked like tendrils of ice were starting to creep forward. He backed away reflexively, and closed the bathroom door.

Had the boiler conked out? He checked: the thermostat was set to 70, and the thermometer in the hall read 70, but why, why did it feel so cold? Ice spun spider web patterns outward from the room's darkest corners, and the frame of the bay window was rimmed with the same dull gray ice.

Gazing with dread at the bay window's frosty mantle, a flicker beyond the window caught his eye. A headlamp from a vehicle in the road. Moving slowly. Then it stopped. Was it...? Yes, by god, it was the mail truck. Jenny's mail truck – he was sure of it.

He was seized with an overwhelming urge to meet her, to thank her, to praise her for making her rounds in this dismal weather.

Although it felt like midnight to him, it was only late afternoon, not yet completely dark. He fumbled on his parka and limped out to the stoop. He swayed there, buffeted by a thousand probing fingers of sleet, and gazed with longing down the steep, whitened driveway.

And there...there! His Jenny, a small figure at the very end of the driveway, stepping gracefully over the barrier of snow pushed up over the entrance by the snow plow. The overgrown cedar trees by the mailbox were heavy with their burden of ice. They slumped toward her, defeated by the storm's ferocity.

He started carefully down the ice-covered steps. A branch snapped with a sound like a gunshot.

Startled, he lost his footing. He grabbed for the railing, but the wood was old and rotten. It split, throwing him off-balance, and his feet slid out from under him. Fire lit up his bum knee, and he screamed.

From the end of the driveway a mittened hand waved gaily.

Gritting his teeth he humped down step by step on his butt until his feet found the pavement. It was a solid slab of ice, slick as a skating rink, treacherous as a woman's smile. He took one tentative step, then another, head down against the wind.

...and fell again, harder this time.

He lay stunned for a moment, gasping in quiet agony. The fall had bruised his cheekbone and opened a cut in his cheek. Probing fingers of sleet stroked his upturned face with cruel caresses. In a moment of clarity he knew he must get back inside, crawling if he had to, and phone for help.

He turned his wet and bleeding face toward the house. Tendrils of gray ice were growing around the doorframe, colonizing the windowsills, reaching out toward him from between the cracks in the old lap siding.

Clarity fled.

He forced himself to stand. The urge to reach Jenny was fierce now, stronger than the pain. The driveway yawned before him, longer and steeper then he remembered. Night was almost here, but the coating of ice glowed dully, reflecting the streetlight far below.

"Come to me!" she cried from the driveway's end.

"I'm coming. Please...wait..."

His plea came out as a whisper, when he had meant to shout. Dragging his injured leg behind him he staggered on. Behind him now, the wind whipped him forward as though it shared his urgency. Exhausted, he sagged against its strength.

The wind turned and pitched him headlong, grinding his body into the unforgiving ice.

"The third time's the charm."

He lifted his head. The figure gazed down at him, expression-less. Her mass of hair -- now auburn, now white gold, now faded by twilight to a dull gray -- writhed like a live thing in the wind. Gusts rose around her, keening high and gleeful.

Through a veil of pain and confusion he saw the face of youthful beauty melding into the beloved, worn face of his wife -- a phantasmagoria, shifting, always shifting. Flesh melted, revealing skull.

"Delores," he said, like a prayer. "I made it. I beat the ice." He shuddered. "I'm hurt. Can you help me?"

The figure began to laugh, Not the gay, tinkling laugh that had charmed him, but a low chuckle. She held out her arms like a mother encouraging her baby to take his first, hesitant steps. Her embrace, terrifying and welcoming, drew him down into the darkness.

Something broke inside of him. It might have been his heart.

After a while, the storm eased and a sickle moon rode the tortured sky. Pale moonlight glinted off shards of ice and the pool of blood turning to crystal on the frozen ground.

THE UNDERFUNDED BOTANICAL GARDEN - RAY HUDSON

I held on to his waist as his moped took a sharp corner past an American GI flashing a peace-sign and a smile. We walked through the botanical garden at the Saigon Zoo, underfunded and shabby,

my hand in his. It was still Saigon.
It was still the war and I had returned.
He was eighteen or nineteen.
I was a few years older. A year earlier,
within the year of highest mortality rates
for American combat troops in Vietnam,

we had started writing to each other. I had been with the 101st Airborne Division. I was a drafted conscientious objector. I was a medic.

On the reverse of a tiny studio photograph
he had inscribed: *I offer you my small picture*
to memory, we lived together in this
summer holiday. Your friend, Văn Thi.

October 25th, 1968. That suggests
we knew each other pretty well. And *that*

seems not only unlikely, but impossible. I didn't even know my-
self. Why I came back when it was still Saigon, it was still the
war, is not important.

There must have been ten-thousand mopeds
in the city. There were at least that many taxis
decorated like Mardi Gras floats. I leaned in
as he circled a grotesque public statue
celebrating the defenders of the corrupt régime,
four-and-a-half years before it was toppled.

The wind on my face, on my arms, in my hair, was sweeter
than cologne. Just days before my year had ended, before I had
headed

"back to the world," back to the States,
orders had come down stipulating
non-judicial punishment for anyone caught

with his sleeves rolled up after sunset,
another command attempt to curb malaria.
I thought of the high grass at Dak To

in the Central Highlands swept by breezes, the grass at the edge
of the aid station at Cu Chi swaying in the wind as evening
shrouded the perimeter,

of bitter nights on guard duty at the edge
of the perimeter and hearing with the first shudder

of morning a breeze begin to make the rounds,
and with each memory the memory of the wind
moving the hairs on my arm recalling me to myself.
And when the promoters of carnage,

the profiteers of rank and casualty denied me this simplest con-
tact with the world, the circumference of my will shrank.

The calendar was blackened. I rolled down
my sleeves fold by fold. I was undone almost
always at such times, spent hours on my cot,
unfeeling, Jesus. The windows

in the French restaurant overlooked the city.
We talked and ate. He seemed incredibly young.

As it grew dark, the glass became opaque and reflected back the
room. The sweet barrage of caramelized onions rose from our
stoneware bowls.

His English was minimal; my Vietnamese,
non-existent. He said he now lived
with his father and that he was studying
to be an engineer. I told him how
when his first letter had arrived outside Cu Chi
the rain had stopped. The war had receded.

The planes were like small bees and the bombing like soft drum-
ming. I didn't tell him about the casualties I had recorded in the
battalion aid station log, traumatic amputations, fragmentation
wounds.

He wanted the war to end. He wanted
to be an engineer. He suggested we meet
at his home at noon the next day and again
visit the botanical gardens before my plane
left that evening. Earlier in the day,
I had been surprised at how few people

escaped to the relative peace of the park in spite of the deterio-
ration of the zoo and the neglect of the gardens. We had walked
down several paths before he reached over for my hand.

I knew this was a customary gesture
to make in Vietnam. I'd seen it on the streets.
But all my Midwest evangelical Lutheran
upbringing shuddered at any public display
of affection and cringed at anything suggesting
love between two men. Which it did, to me

but not to him. I knew that. I knew he was expressing only
friendship. I took his hand. "Another walk through the gardens
would be great," I said.

But my flight was rescheduled and there was time
only to rush to his house in a taxi, give him
a quick goodbye, make a speedy bow of respect
to his father, and head to the airport. The American
War in Vietnam is history and we are back
pumping up tourism. I like to think

my intentions were good. That throughout the expanse of time
and space, as Buddhism teaches,

I tried to do good. That for as long as
that strange and violent world existed, I tried
to dispel misery. But I was just another
American whose contact with a young
Vietnamese became a liability. Did he finish
his studies and become an engineer?

Did he avoid the draft as the Army of the Republic of South Viet-
nam became increasingly desperate for bodies? Did he survive
the fall of Saigon in 1975? Was he able to destroy my letters,

    evidence of close association with the enemy
    because that's what I was, what I became,
    what I always had been. Did he emerge
    reformed from a reeducation camp? As I turned
    from his porch to the taxi, he promised
    to write. I promised to be faithful.

BLOOD IN THE WATER: TOO MUCH TRANSPIRED - KAREN KISH

November 4, 2006
Budapest, Hungary

I slide the delicate lace curtain aside to absorb the stunning view. Directly across looms the Museum of Applied Arts, the Art Nouveau masterpiece with its regally intricate, green-gold Zolnay-tiled roof. To the left is the famed circular Corvin Cinema, headquarters of the 1956 Hungarian Revolution. Facing the theater is the opposing Kilian Barracks, '56 headquarters of the Hungarian Armored Division. A contrasting ideological trio of art, cinema, and the dual, dark faces of iron-fisted communism.

I turn back into our dinner party of six. "This apartment has been in my family for three generations." Andras sweeps his arm toward the lofty corniced ceiling, burnished hardwoods, gracefully aging furnishings, all in privileged, Old World style.

Andras invites the six of us toward the laden dinner table. "And now for our humble repast."

Wine flutes and silver cutlery mingle with our lively getting-to-know-you conversation. Andras, Gabor, and Kata with stories about their university students and colleagues. Kati, Andras's wife and a representative to the European Union Parliament, details incentives to aid Roma gypsies. My husband Sandy and I add anecdotes about our global high school students at the American International School of Budapest.

And yet a doleful spirit softly whispers around the table: *Today is the day. Fifty years ago today.* The day that 1,000 Russian tanks shrieked down this same stately Üllöi út to strangle Budapest with the vicious finality of the Soviet hammer.

As the only non-Hungarian at the table, I study these elite intellectuals, including full-blooded Sandy, and wonder what memories they have of the '56 Revolution, of forty years of life under the Soviet regime of the Iron Curtain, of restrictions, lies, betrayals, and everyday terrors.

And then, with goblets lifted for a dessert *Egészsegedre!*, Gabor poses the inevitable question. "What do you remember about November 4th, 1956?" The 'to your health' toast is silenced. Everyone instantly pensive about that day of infamy - and the preceding twelve days of battle.

October 23, 1956

Inspired by a Polish workers' uprising a few months earlier, Budapest Technical University students drafted a daring 16-point manifesto, including demands for multi-party elections, freedom of speech, a living wage, expulsion of Russian troops from Hungary, reinstatement of ousted Imre Nagy as premier. A first wave of thousands of students marched to the statue of Józef Zachariasz Bem, a Polish general and expatriate hero of the Hungarian Revolution of 1848 against the Austrian Habsburgs.

The story goes...On the way to Bem Square, they passed a clinic with a young nurse waving a national flag from an upstairs window. When raucous boos erupted at the mandated Soviet symbol emblazoned in the center, she ducked inside, cut out the emblem, and returned to wave the Hungarian colors with a hole in the center. Raving cheers greeted the altered banner as inspired pocket knives ripped to free their flags from the renounced Soviet wheat sheaves and hammer.

The second inflamed wave of student rebels marched, shouting and singing, to the statue of Sándor Pétofi, the martyred poet whose prophetic "Rise, Hungarians" verse inspired the 1848 revolt: "This we swear, this we swear, we will be slaves no more."

Both protest groups coalesced at Parliament, where the crowd burgeoned to an angry, chanting mob of 100,000. "Nagy! Nagy! Nagy!" Panicked, officials produced feckless, deposed Nagy, who, from the balcony, feebly addressed the incensed crowd as "comrades" and told them to go home.

Enraged, one contingent broke from the mass and streamed to *Hösök tér*, Heroes' Square. Steel ropes, acetylene torches, and hammers decimated the despised, fifty-foot-high Stalin statue in an hour, leaving only the tyrant's boots with a defiant, scissored rebel flag in the heel.

Enraged, a second contingent stormed the state radio station with an ultimatum: broadcast their manifesto or be attacked. Police fatally fired into the unarmed crowd, and after hours of fierce fighting, the rebels seized control of the station. Sixteen died, with one martyr wrapped in a Hungarian flag and hoisted aloft in somber victory.

October 24 - 29, 1956

For six days the freedom fighters roiled the city's streets, resisting against Russian tanks and machine guns with homemade gasoline bombs, oxygen tank projectiles, trolley cars as battering rams, snipped electrical wires electrocuting Soviet soldiers inside their tanks.

An ambushed civilian throng of thousands at the Parliament building was surrounded by snipers and tanks firing directly into defenseless men, women, and children, massacring hundreds.

Until, on October 29th, eerie silence prevailed. Imre Nagy, now prime minister, brokered a truce with the Soviets. Krushchev withdrew his troops from Hungary.

But *sssshhhhh!,* here's Kruschev's secret: those Russian tanks rumbled only to the border. To wait for reinforcements. And for the moment to arrest Nagy.

October 30 - November 4, 1956

Victory! Countrywide euphoria. Political groups formed freely; newspapers were printed and posted on lamp posts; jubilant new lives emerged. Russian bookstores were destroyed, Soviet war memorials vandalized, infuriating red stars on buildings shattered. One implacable Iron Curtain country had broken the back of the Soviet monster.

For five days.

And then, early on November 4th, Operation Whirlwind's 1,000 Russian tanks shrieked down Andras's stately Üllöi út to fatally strangle Budapest. While the world simply watched.

For the next three days, the Soviet artillery, infantry, and air strikes pummeled the freedom fighters, joined by Hungarian army defectors. Russian tanks meticulously blasted the ground floor of every rebel hideout, one after another, until they collapsed, leaving the city pocked with bitter rubble. The final tally: 2,500 rebel patriots dead, 20,000 wounded.

By November 7th this wayward Soviet satellite's bloodied knuckles were resoundingly rapped as the Iron Curtain crashed down once again with agonizing finality.

* * *

Gabor's question still lingers, insistent. *"What do you remember about November 4th, 1956?"*

Andreas leans forward and begins. "I was only seven years old. But I remember hearing the thunderous noise of the tanks moving by here on November 4th — it felt like for hours. The next day a burned-out Russian tank smoldered right out front, for three days. Its chilling imprint mocked us for ten years." He raises his hands for a decade of emphasis.

Kata gazes toward that image beyond the window. "November 4 changed my life forever. My father was in Prague, so my mother and I huddled in our flat, terrified, listening to the groan of tanks charging down our street — and stopping right at our house. The Kilian Barracks was across the street; that was their target. But it was empty, so they rolled on." She shudders in retrospective relief.

Gabor nods toward his wife in thoughtful assent. "It changed my life forever too. My mother left the day before to visit her sister in Australia. Her visa was for three months, but for three years she tried to arrange for us to emigrate. Eventually, the Hungarian government gave permission for my sister and me to leave, but not my father. So she returned here in 1959." He rests his heavy-hearted head in his hands.

Kati has a different perspective. "I was too young to remember much about the uprising itself, but I have a clear memory of those five days of freedom. Everyone was in the streets, euphoric: smiling, happy, singing, chains broken."

Andras echoes her memory. "Yes, I remember that euphoria.

Just five days. And then, in 1991, when the last Russian tanks finally left Hungary, there was relief — but no euphoria. By then, too much had transpired." He lowers his head in resignation.

Sandy was also seven years old on that day, but in a Hungarian community in Norwalk, Connecticut, far from the battlefield. He fingers his silver dessert fork, feeling removed from the immediacy. "I was so far away and so young. But I do remember my parents worried about their relatives. I heard the news on the radio, echoing with bombs and gunfire. I was scared."

As for me, being neither in Hungary then, nor Hungarian, it's history to me, a profoundly ruthless history learned, until now, only from a textbook. I absorb these faces that have been through "too much."

The Aftermath

Sandy has a vivid personal memory of the immediate aftermath: watching the notorious 1956 Summer Olympics semi-final water polo match between the Soviet Union and Hungary, held just weeks after November 4th. Mrs. Szűcs, proud owner of the biggest TV screen on Soundview Avenue, invited Sandy's entire neighborhood to cram into her living room and watch what would become the Blood in the Water duel, the most famous water polo match in history.

As defending gold medal champions, the Hungarians had managed easy victories in the round robin matches in Melbourne — and faced Russia in the semi-final.

Seething with fury for their country, the men entered the pool, braced for a crusade for freedom. A sport known for violent kicks and body blows, the match quickly devolved into a brutal brawl spurred on by 8,000 Cold War sympathizers and Hungarian expats shouting *"Hajra Magyarok!"* Go, Hungarians!

The taunting Magyars netted a goal. Then another. Then two more. With one minute left, the score was 4 - 0 Hungary.

And then, with the ball on the opposite end of the pool, a penalty whistle blew. Hungary's Ervin Zador turned toward the signal, then back - as Russian Valentin Prokopov savagely smashed his face. Blurry blood dripped into the water as Zador swam to the edge of the pool. A coach motioned him away. *No, no, swim to the other side where the TV camera is.* So Zador swam, streaming blood, straight into the TV camera, straight into the world's conscience.

Sandy remembers Mrs. Szűcs's living room during the match, all eyes on the television, a constant chant of *"Ria, Ria Hungaria!"* At the moment of victory, everyone rose, fists raised, bellowing riotous revenge.

Zador scored two goals and thirteen stitches for the deep gash under his eye. He was benched, but the Hungarians still won gold against Yugoslavia. An eye for an eye - the only weapon left in Hungary's cowed arsenal.

* * *

Seventeen years later, in 1973 during our Eurail honeymoon, Sandy and I spotted a fantastical poster in the Vienna American Express office: Spend a Weekend in Budapest. *Behind the Iron Curtain!*

As euphoric as an idyllic return to the fatherland seemed on a poster, the reality of our weekend was stark. One hour of free time outside, trailed by a black-cloaked agent. Austro-Hungarian Empire once-majestic buildings bomb-blasted black. A handful of cars, all black, a handful of dark-hued pedestrians. A store with a mostly bare, splintered plywood shelf and a forlorn toy Sputnik futilely whirling from the ceiling. We walked to the riverbank, wished we had scraps for the scrawny pecking pigeons, sat on a decaying bench, stared at the bleak Danube.

But we were in Hungary for only two days. For Hungarians, the aftermath of Andras's "too much" spanned three shadowy decades of vengeful Soviet puppetry.

* * *

Leaving Andras and Kati's genteel flat, Sandy and I stroll by a covey of plump, pecking pigeons, past imperial buildings sandblasted back to their glory. We stop at the *villamos megálló* and wait for the tram with colorfully cloaked Hungarians. Above us the Chain Bridge string of lights winks at the Danube that once flowed blood.

I've stood next to the bronzed shoes lining that riverbank, once filled with Jews executed by the soulless Hungarian Arrow Cross militia as the river bled red. I've touched the Soviets' bullet holes scarring the Parliament's grand buildings. I've descended into the '56 Memorial Underground Museum, rooted in front of a tattered Hungarian flag with its empty center, proudly mounted on a rough brick wall, and willed it: *tell me your stories.*

On the tram I listen to the drift of cheerful banter and absorb these faces, knowing that, beneath those facades, a dreadful spectre still whispers a reflexive, fearful alert to everyone of a certain generation.

Because far too much has transpired.

TO MY POSTCARD COLLECTION
- TRICIA KNOLL

You don't want to hear that fleeting
word—*email.* You know
every story has two sides,
even *wish you were here, I miss you,*
or *thank you for your kindness over tea.*
You bear extra-special images of antique
roses, Wyoming's wonky jackalope,
Inuit line drawing of whales, the photos
of motorized skates or Escher's waterfall
from the Museum of Impractical Devices.
I love your flimsiness inviting
my right hand to scrawl with no fear
of the fingerprint of delete.
Go ahead—invite the mail carrier
to flip you like a pancake
destined for a drool of maple syrup.
My scribble intrigues those
who approach hard-knock mail slots
and arched sheet-metal boxes, wary
of the mad dog, to sling ads
for grocer's sales or water bills.

OLD BOOKS - PETER SNOW

smell bad, and shed
bus tickets, forgotten postcards.

Packed tight on unreachable shelves
they develop liver spots
gather spiderdust
and creep away to die.

They are for those
who say *slightly foxed*
without humor;
those who use such words as
frontispiece, colophon,
endpapers, even in coffeeshops,
surrounded by others
with laptops and smartphones.

Yet in the corner, peering through
thick spectacles at a print newspaper,
a customer sees another leafing through
one such dry, rustling corpse,
and nods in solemn recognition
at the act of resuscitation.

ACCIDIA - PETER SNOW

I heard the blackbird sing
in the orchard before the rain set in.

This apple calms my mind
as the rain butt fills.

My worries and anxieties
soak into the ground;

the dull drip drip of the tap
soothes my senses. Eyelids droop.

The world is like a picture
under tissue paper in an old book.

Shouldn't the hour have chimed,
chasing necessity through the house?

The spring was wound so tight
the clock stopped, the key lost.

The cat shivers under the dripping bush.
But I am not spurred to move.

Steam rises from my cup.
I bite the apple again.

HOW I HANG ON - MALISA GARLIEB

Not sure, I replied.
When the rain stopped,
I took my gray body on
a gray walk. It mostly
cooperated.

I saw a pink flower in the grass
and counted the petals:
somehow, pentagrams reassure.

(We were careful with one another.)

I took herbs, naps, gulps of air.
I clutched pillows like driftwood,
their silk a substitute for skin.

(I'm ready to admit I wanted more.)

This is boring. It isn't a poem.
Only a way to kill a few minutes.
I write it, you read it—done.

Now what?

I had notions of planting
a yellow garden.
Marigold makes a soothing balm
and buttercups are nice.
But rot happens regardless.

(I asked him to hold me all night,
however he still could.)

I'm not convinced any of this
matters, yet
I write it down.

(I told the doctors
he was gone,
but they kept going.)

And I took off my rings.

ON THE PLAYGROUND - ANN FISHER

Swings

On the playground, Sammy stands with the small group of boys as much as he stands alone. They huddle in their black hoodies near the swings, but no one dares to touch the childish things. They are in sixth grade now, after all. They gather at the farthest point they can, pushing the edge of the rule, causing the duty teacher to lift her head from her watch to scrutinize them, cast a dark scowl in their general direction.

Sammy could care less. He drags his hand through his thick bushy hair, lets it drop back to the screen on his phone, thumbs flying. The only part of him that is a blur of action. He has already mastered the art of leaving his body standing there without being fully inside. He is a 12-year-old dotted with skull motifs on his sweatshirt uniform, shoulders slumped carefully into the curve of "don't care." The others ignore him, think he doesn't notice or hear their talk; they are used to seeing him head bent, canopy of hair protecting his precious phone.

Sammy responds to his mother's text with quick, practiced digits. She is fierce in her mothering, propelling him with a mammary vise grip he can't unlock. Her texts demand too, so he never lets the phone out of sight. It connects her to him, and he'd be lost without it. She is the only thing that sometimes keeps his brothers off of him, the only one who steps in and yells something different. And she signs him out of school when his belly aches from clenching.

He texts her during spelling, when he should be making sense of the vowels that seem to rebel against his pencil, the letters teaming up against him. He doesn't care about the teacher's marks checking off the pages, scratching his careless work with thin red lines. They match the scratches on his face- from the family dogs, he says. Dogs that bite his cheekbones, knock him down, create limps and hobbles he carries to school and explains away. A few times, his armor has slipped, an opening he can't control, and his stepfather's name ekes out before he closes up the gap. Loyalty has a way of suturing breaches. Sammy's teachers wonder if the twisted words meant what they don't want to comprehend.

In 2nd grade, Sammy took care of it all by keeping his head on his desk, one ear pressed to the fake wood top, eyes open and seeing. He moved listlessly, as if hurrying to his yellow coat hanging in his cubby could make too many waves in his fragile world and set danger in motion. Time slowed and events faltered while Sammy dragged his feet across the pock-marked classroom floor. Still, he missed nothing. He watched everything with his watery green eyes, trained well in a war zone.

He keeps an eye on it all now, too. Takes in everything in a quick dart of glance, hair masquerading as mask, providing cover for the stealth that is necessary. When all this vigilance weighs him down, he misses days just like when he was little. The school doesn't seem to care, slumped like him, they've given up. Sammy knows it has a lot to do with his mother, who will barge in the principal's office, eyes flaring, tear them to pieces with her sharp tongue and threats. They try to appease her, just like he does. Easier to flow quietly along behind her.

In an opposite attack but to the same purpose, Sammy keeps adults at a distance through his honed and sophisticated manners. Politeness and feigned respect are his big guns, the ones that keep everyone looking the other way. Just as he needs them to do. He doesn't miss a beat; he has a way of wrapping his politeness around each teacher like a video game controller, buttons clicking in his seemingly innocent hands. He wriggles out of work, out of school, out of class while teachers look on. He charms them out of their rule books, uses thoughtful words to erase their red pen across his non-existent work.

Sammy hides the weight of family behind all that hair and the large billed cap. Compelled to move his thumbs across the keyboard. "I have to text her back," he states, picking through her communications to decipher the future. Often, she picks him up, takes him away from school, with a moment's notice. He scans her texts to find out her next step. Then he calculates his.

The teachers talk behind closed doors. Calls to the state are marked "unsubstantiated"; calls home leave them battered and bruised. Sammie's mother lacerates them, cages them with names of lawyers, the eternal threat to sue. She tells them one excuse or another about why he isn't attending: doctors' offices, allergy visits, x-rays, medication. She has diagnosed him with ADHD and the doctors prescribe freely. Ritalin and Adderall, pills and capsules he never sees. Between her rage and his manners, there exists a truth no one can see. They try to educate this boy, wrapped in printed patterned bones and eyeless sockets.

Near the swings, his phone lights the information he needs to survive the afternoon, the evening, never mind the afternoon. Sammy reads her texts. Stands absolutely still, a swing hanging heavy at its fulcrum.

Climbing Dome

Louis's seams are about to rip. Not the physical ones, tying together his t-shirts and khakis and carefully laced shoes. He is happiest when all four loops are equal and they are, today. But along his skin, the tiny seams that hold him together bulge with panic. He sits on top of the rubber-coated metal of the dome, alone, floating above the smiles and screams and tag games below him.

He waits for the just- right feeling to find him. And when it eludes him, he pushes his red glasses farther into his worried face and waits for it to pull him under. The chaos. The wrongness that surrounds him everywhere he goes. It finds him as he sits on the white stool connected to the pull-out lunch tables, taunts him as he sits alone, full of worry. It sits with him at the top of the dome, empty air his only companion.

They move away when he speaks. His mother explains that he is special, that the others are jealous of his intelligence, his orderly math pages, the way he understands things they don't — like how electricity works. His mother's words both soothe and sear. If she tells the truth, then he is lost. If she is lying, merely saying nice things to make him feel better, then he knows he can never be found.

He looks down, sees them playing that game again. The one that can only be played in his proximity. The playground lady sees them below, too, he knows this for a fact without having to look at her. He likes to imagine that she does not know about the game. But that may be a lie, too. The game where they wipe their hands across each other's arms and backs, shouting "now YOU'VE got it!" And the one wearing the imaginary stuff makes a face of disgust and fear, runs to wipe it off on the next classmate. The game they call "Wipe". Or "You've got the Louis touch".

If the teachers ever heard them, they would think of cooties, and cootie catchers, origami folded pain perched on small stubby fingers. He knows about those things, too. But this is a different game, and Louis knows being the center of it is a bad thing. But he can't figure out how he got there, or how to extricate himself. Extricate is usually a good word. He can feel it pull the back of his tongue to the roof of his mouth. He says the word ten times, like usual. Then once backward. Etacirtxe. When he says it backward, he lets the c turn soft in his mouth, like a snake's hiss. Softens the hard "a" so it sounds foreign. Like the subtitled films he watches with his mom on the weekends.

Louis says the wrong thing almost every time. He knows his thoughts can't come out any other way, but he wishes his words and sentences would come apart before they find their way out of his mouth. They fall out like train wrecks, causing other kids to scatter. He spends the rest of recess sifting through the wreckage, desperate to understand, holding tight to the bars of the dome so he won't fall off. He watches them move below him like tigers under his cage. Circling. He squeezes his right hand on the blue bar, his left on the yellow. Then repeats. This, he knows how to do. He doesn't know what to tell the teacher. Or his mother. He does not want to be the thing that can catch on you, like a disease. He knows he shouldn't cry. Reporting and crying increase their speed, their swiping and running from the imaginary him. He knows it's better to stay up here ticking the time away at the top of the dome, floating as far above it as he can.

Sandbox

Livie lords over the sandbox, the tiny square of wood left over from her parent's school days, with the poison pressure-treated wood barely able to hold in the old wet sand. The other girls bend to her will, then run to tell on her when she bosses them, kicks in their castles and stupid little villages.

"Livie knocked down my fairy town!" They yell to the teacher. When she is called over, Livie walks the walk, head down, chubby cheeks slack and a pout pinned to her ruby red lips.

"Did not!" Always Livie's first words. "It was my castle, Miss Lightner. I built it."

Livie is full of something she wishes wasn't true. Her want-ings have wound themselves into truths and they press into hard blocks, building something she wants everyone to see. "I drew that" she will tell the teacher, pointing proudly to an art piece hanging by the 6th grade classrooms. "Isn't it nice?" She forces the teachers to build the fantasy with her; confused, they let the statements stand and do not challenge her. It fills her hunger for a moment, letting her bounce and twirl down the hall as if she were a real kindergartener.

Livie is fire. Her body spins and spins when she is supposed to be criss-cross applesauce, spoons in the bowl. She barges and bumps her way across the classroom, jumping in front of the other kindergarteners when they are cuter or quieter, the adults bending down with smile umbrellas, leaving her out in pouty rain. Livie stomps when she is angry, writes scrawled illegible howling letters to teachers if they have given other little chil-dren too much of their love. That kind of attention scares her, leaves her so worried she has to bellow with anger, tell everyone "I'm MAD at you!" and stomp away. For safety.

She has figured out that adults listen when she tells half-truths. They lean in with pursed lips but see only her when they are trying to sort out what is real from what might be a Livie lie. Livie likes this, when adults have their faces turned toward her and her alone. But she gets that feeling in her belly, too. The one that feels like she will throw up from being so hungry. So she stomps and bellows to cover it up and she is sent away again. It used to be the Time Out Corner. Now, they call it "Livie's Place".

Livie's clothes are tight against her too-round body. She is always eating, sometimes things slipped from superman or unicorn lunch boxes. Sometimes, things the others drop on the floor. Something is threatening to get out of her and she threatens her classmates to keep it in. Bossy, hands on hips, blonde hair bouncing angrily at her cheeks, she tells the boys to "Move it. Now." And they do. Livie's big blue eyes lord over the others and she likes it. Groups automatically part when she barges into the dress-up corner, or the number bench. They quickly place whatever she wants- headphones, books, puzzle pieces - into her demanding outstretched hands. They step back with big-pupiled eyes like Livie's cat when she dresses it up in little doll's clothes. Her classmates, barely reading, can see what adults cannot. And Livie knows what they see. She bosses them to block it out.

"That's not real! Bunnies don't talk" and when reminded to keep quiet for the story, she gets louder because then, they see her. Sitting in her chair outside the group, she pouts outwardly but inside, she glows. She is not so lost when the teachers scowl and worry and the kids squeeze glances at her from out of their circle.

For a kindergartener, Livie is too full of things she shouldn't know. For instance, she already knows how to spell, so she refuses to put the letters into the same order as the others do with their thick pencils and big pink erasers. "It's for babies," Livie exclaims, then has to walk again to the thinking chair. She distracts herself in the math station because she is busy calculating which children will put up a fight when she takes things from their cubbies and which ones will shake their heads "no" when the teacher asks "does Livie have something of yours?"

"I am smarter than the teachers," she tells the little boy next to her in circle time. Because they can't seem to teach about real things, like how terrible it feels to be tricked. Or what to do with that feeling that burns inside, making tummies wobbly and puddles pool in her little chair like hot shame.

After recess, Livie will tell that story again, the one about an uncle who hangs her up by her pants and leaves her there for days. Wide eyed, her peers will run to the teachers, repeating the tales. They don't want stories like that spinning inside them, either. Livie watches them intently as they run to tattle. When the teacher questions, Livie flashes her toothy smile. Erases the whole picture with a "that's not true". She will launch into another story that will make sure the only answer is that Livie is a liar. Her family owns a candy store with lollipops as big as kitties. She'll launch into the story of her uncle again. Only this time, he will be floating off into the sky underneath a gi-nor-mous balloon he bought her at the fair.

And some moments, Livie will get the threads mixed up, like the letters in the alphabet when they can't hold onto their sing-song melody. Sentences will fall apart and come back together again against her will. She will look adults in the eye and state, "I am a bad girl". And she'll know it isn't a lie. Then quickly, as if new words could gobble up what has slipped out, Livie will tell a story about driving a car in her backyard. She will say she can run faster than anyone, brag that she knows how to fly high in the sky all the way to the moon. And the teacher will ask, "Livie, do you wish that was true?"

Livie will whisper just soft enough so no one can hear. "I wish. I really do."

***

Soon, recess will be over. The children will stream in from the grounds as the red and white megaphone amplifies the next direction. "Line Up!" Louis will straighten his socks so the seams do not beg his attention, climb carefully down from safety. Sammie will survey the parking lot for his mother's dark blue car, plan his next move based on how much gravel shoots up when she spins around the curve. Livie will throw sand at Charlotte and then run to stand in line, back straight, eyes locked forward, one of the good girls.

Inside the classroom, they will be asked to complete their worksheets. Study vocabulary. Learn to write in complete sentences. Later, they will be asked to solve for unknowns; calculate missing angles. The state will require standardized tests to measure the depth and breadth of their knowledge. Skilled teachers will coax them to pay attention as best they can, knowing they have other, more important, exams to master.

THE YELLOW WALLPAPER* - ELISABETH BLAIR

The title of an 1892 short story by Charlotte Perkins Gilman

I met him when he was 14

we'd both been shipped off to a
cult-based lockdown for "troubled teens"

I from neglect and solitude
he from catastrophic abuse

he killed himself at 33

but before that—in his 20s—
he called me crying
I'd never heard him cry
he said he wanted to quit being

a white supremacist—
he'd seen a movie in which
somebody was showing someone
something beautiful and he said
I think there's art in me

I think there's art in me
                                    and I didn't
                            help him or couldn't
                            help him or he didn't
                            know how to ask or I
                                didn't know how
                                    to offer
I have a video of us at that place
he's 15 and we're on stage
he'd just stood up after being
pushed around in a wheelchair
for a week as a "challenge"
the audience is clapping
the camera zooms in and he looks
sideways at it — right at the lens—
and I can see everything ahead of him—

                                the fight with his father
                                the shot fired
                                the prison sentence
                                the gang
                                the organized hate
                                the phone call
                                (I couldn't or didn't help)
                                marriagechildrensuicide

in the video he's
                    busy
we all were—
navigating the labyrinthine
yellow wallpaper
and he couldn't or didn't—

on the phone he stopped crying and said

> *are you God*
> *are you the Light*
> *we should be together*
> *give me your address*
> *I'll get a Greyhound bus*
> *so what if you have a boyfriend*
> *you're not married to him*
> *what if you're the answer to all this*

sometimes one of us
becomes an island—
the only place to land
for a thousand thousand miles

> if I was a shitty island
> it wasn't my fault

I was

> busy

we all are— trying to remember
     whether to hate ourselves
          or everyone else—

in the video we're bowing
he looks at the camera and I can see him
                being hunted

          —I know he evaded that
          predator until he was 33

STROKE - ELISABETH BLAIR

in the kitchen, between racks
of jars and mess from lunch,
within the automatic
alert in which she
outlined her days,

within the cologne of grief
and banality, she crossed the floor,
feet nested in slippers
hand-sewn, essential

lifted both arms, dress
with the sleeves,
body reaching—

she reached—

ceramic knob in her fingers

she reached,
     stayed reaching,
lips trembling,
one side more than the other

so that the ocean met the shore
at an angle—and all was well
—all was well—*fire in the hole*
            —all was well—

THE CRITIC - KRISTIN LAFOLLETTE

I'm not the killer of animals.

I think
         I've had no part in this,
no blood

on my hands.

Our community, a unified body, but
even Judas hanged himself—
No time for redemption,

a thing like money, a wet paper
smell, bills scattered on a sidewalk
flooded with rainwater.

People's faces become like gauze
as my eyes change, the left one and then the right—
I know these people, their bodies make
the shapes of arrows

when their gazes settle upon me.

My skin is different, but the same—
        I am the woman they wish to ignore.

I am the woman whose glassy voice disappears
when I open my mouth;

I chew words down,
a story told backward,
bright and broken like
the delicate filaments
of clouds.

GOLDEN SHOVEL: NO DOUBT
HE THOUGHT OF EVERYTHING
– CANDELIN WAHL

(after Mary Oliver, "The Buddha's Last Instruction")

Beloved boy-man, too cocky to say no,
engorged his veins with self-doubt.
I wear a mother's shame for times he,
with mounds of talent, thought
to test his body, line it with shards of
glass, prove immunity to everything
liquid, powder, bright wiggle worms that
flash-panned the ache—but had to be had.
The scene on repeat, the whoosh of it happened,
bruises like Rorschachs bled patchwork in
his forearms, satanic tattoos draped his
bony shoulders. He crept a minefield of difficult
truths—to save his one precious life.

WOMAN ON FIRE # 4 - SHARON LOPEZ MOONEY

I cleaned house
pulled out furniture of memories not moved in dog years
wiped up spilled disappointment crusted in corners
couches back I vacuumed crumbs and caked on tears
from under cushions of affection

I sorted, bagged and trashed
each smelly argument, lie, promise, stuffing
black bags, some slit from sharp edges,
drawers of shared secrets upside down,
recollection shelves emptied, wiped off

I combed through framed memories
taped torn portraits
realign snapshots cradled in plastic sleeves
pulled down boxes of songs, dances and laughter
to be catalogued and stowed deep in the basement

I stood in the middle of my new milieu
carefully laid as proof,
an invitation to resolve,

your aroma erased by a hint of myrrh
your touch peeled from my flesh pink from scrubbing

A knock and a whistle calls from the porch
I turn, latch on to what I believed to be gone
but there you are, a relaxed smile, casually leaning on
your banister of charm, scent of seduction
not needing to speak, patient, you, ready to light a fire.

THE MYRIAD WAYS THE CONCUBINES PLEASED THE SULTAN - KELLIE FLEURY

She opened the box, though her father forbade it.

It sat on the periphery of Father's round tower, serene and foreboding, exhilarating in its obduracy. Its blue sides conjured the seas around Corfu, the lid invoked the unfathomable sapphire of the dome of heaven with its multitudinous, riotous stars. Like the midnight sky, the box was studded with constellations, but these were unfamiliar to her, though her father was an astronomer and she had learned the Pleiades from Cassiopeia long before she could pronounce their names. The stars on high were facile, effervescent. The stars on the box were less sprightly – brass and gilt, some to hold the box together, some describing inscrutable incantations.

As she grew, so did the box. It always measured itself against the height of her knees; chubby with baby fat, scabbed from girlhood misadventures, stubbly with the growth of womanly hair. The box never gathered dust, though it never moved from its shadowy post in Father's observatory, hunkering on the warped wooden floorboards under a colossal tapestry of the known world. The fringe of the tapestry shyly stroked its beetle-browed lid. The box never moved, yet she unfailingly bruised her tender shins on its verdigrised corners, raked her toes on its unyielding feet, snagged her skirts on its grasping hasps. The box conducted its clandestine, smoldering affair with the tapestry of the world, fixed by its own aura, yet still it roved like a rogue moon, crept like a fog, sought her like a blue panther with brass eyes. She knew the box wanted her.

The box smelled old. The box smelled like the oars of ancient pirates, of brine and kelp. The box smelled like the market – cinnamon and myrrh, pepper and turmeric; the musk of the whores and horses; chrysanthemum and frangipani in temples and on supper tables. The box's luscious, lascivious scent undulated and gyrated, was viscous, like the air above a bier on a frigid night. If she spent too long contemplating the oxbloods and marigolds and persimmons and sages of the thick-piled rug that supplicated before the box, her intoxicated thoughts would float from her ears and tear ducts like soap bubbles in a breeze. She would feel as loose and ephemeral as the hookah smoke from the sailors' bars. The box – tender, unwavering, ravishing – was trying to seduce her.

At night, the box stood up, wrapped his naked blue-and-bronze-studded skin in the tapestry of the world – or with the rug of life's hues, if he was feeling very hungry – and came to her in her bed. As a child, he played dolls with her, his voice and form small and commensurate with her own. He was a lively playmate with clever games and fantastic adventures. When she was a girl, he changed his voice and shape to appear as a confidant and with her bemoaned parental unfairness or lamented the spurning by the fishmonger's black-eyed son. When she became a young woman, he took no shape, but crept into her white bed with the susurration of ocean surf, cats' purrs, crickets' arias in tall, summer grasses. He was damp, he smelled of lightning, his breath was ermine and silk. He did not touch her. She told him everything. His lapis throat stayed closed.

Under his tutelage, she grew impervious so that his attacks no longer hurt her, nor did anyone else's. She was wiser than any vizier; she knew the price of ambergris in Damascus; how much camel dung the pyramid men burned while they sipped Pharaoh's ale in the spent, purple dusk; the myriad ways the concubines pleased the sultan. She knew the constellations of this sky and many others. She was impossibly beautiful, but no suitor pleased her. She, having only known the box, knew only how to rebuff them. Her alabaster throat stayed closed.

ABRAM AND THE DUG WELL -
BEN JOHNSON

In Blount County, Alabama, the sun pushes down from above while the waterlogged air ensures no evaporating sweat will cool you. In 1906, my grandfather Abram's mind wasn't on the water in the air but the water under the dirt he was standing on. Of particular interest to him was how far he and his father were going to have to dig before they found that water. He was 15 that year, and the fact that he was only just now in the third grade was not out of the ordinary. At that time and in that county, there were no particular ages associated with different grades. Blount County was subsistence farming country. Children went to school as work allowed; their education simply proceeded along when their need to work in the fields didn't.

The old well had run dry, giving up only brackish mud now. Abram and his father needed to dig a new one. The procedure was simple: pick up a shovel; start digging; stop when you hit water. Some wells in the area could go down fifty feet. Abram didn't wonder how many days it would take to dig the well. He knew the answer. It would take one day from start to finish, even if that day had two sunrises and two sunsets. They weren't going back to the house until they found water. That was his father's way. They would take turns digging until they got the job done.

With a square-point sharpshooter shovel, Abram's father cut a four-foot circle in the sod.

In Blount County, what we now call the social safety net was family. Easy credit with rational terms was not available. Social Security, WIC, TANF, SSDI, and SSRI had not even been imagined. They paid for their food, furniture, house, and much of the farm equipment with the labor they spent farming. They grew and made for themselves what they could, but some things they had to buy, and that meant they had to grow a cash crop to sell. Their cash crop was cotton.

The first hour of digging a well was not the hardest by a long way, but it was the first hour and it had its own work. Your muscles were fresh, you were digging at the surface, but you were also taking the first discouraging steps on a long journey downward. Abram needed to step out of time as he knew it and step into an eternal now without the minutes that marked nothing except the slow progression as that round patch of grass near the cottonwood trees became a deep black void that ended in water.

When his father began to dig, Abram was surprised and discouraged at his father's aggressive pace that seemed more angry than impatient. When faced with a job like that, another person might take the long view and settle into a sustainable pace that a man could keep up for many hours.

A wellhole cannot accommodate two diggers. When they could dig no deeper standing on the grass, Abram's father stepped down into the hole and continued shoveling. They'd spell each other every half hour, one clamoring up, the other hopping down. When the bottom was almost too far down for his father to throw the dirt up and out, Abram handed him a large tin bucket and line. It took about a minute to haul up the bucket weighing about fifty pounds, empty it and send it down again, which gave the digger a quick break to catch his breath and straighten his back.

At some point after the noon meal they had dug the pit deep enough that Abram had to stand on the overturned bucket in order to reach his father's hand and climb up out of the wellhole. After that, only his father dug. Abram ran the bucket up and down until it hurt to open and close his fingers and his shoulders felt leaden and stiff. He was amazed that father was still sending up buckets of dirt as fast as Abram could haul them up and empty them. By the time the sun was touching the tops of the cottonwoods behind them, he was pulling up the fifty-pound bucket about fifteen feet to the surface. Once he returned the bucket, looking into the mouth of the pit, all he could see was the blue of father's shirt when he straightened up and turned with the shovel to load the next fifty pounds of dirt.

"Ready!" his father would shout in an odd, disembodied voice.

"Coming down!" Abram would answer as he sent the bucket back. As he watched his thoughts of supper and sleep disappear with the bucket down that black hole, he recalled as a distant memory that very morning when he had no notion they were going to spend an eternity digging a hole in the ground. That's the way it was, working with father. They were both engaged in a fierce and wearisome contest against the elements, against mechanical failure, against human frailty, against their own desire to just be done with it. Because he worked with his father all day, six days a week, he knew that only vigilance, back-breaking work and orneriness kept the farm going.

Abram had been using the scraps of time while his father dug to build a ladder. Among the lumber left from other projects he found a board ten inches wide and several short lengths of lumber in assorted sizes approximately six inches long. He nailed each of the short pieces to the long board. When finished, Abram slid the ladder down the well. It offered only very shallow steps to climb, but it would do.

The last of the sunlight was fading when Abram's father sent him to the house for a lantern. When he returned, Abram began pulling the bucket up. It wasn't full. By its weight, it had only a couple shovelfuls of dirt in it. He quickly made a lark's head around the lantern's handle with rope and lowered it into the well. He called out for his father, then screamed for him, then screamed at him, and then just screamed as his father's slack form appeared in the pool of light, collapsed kneeling at the bottom of the well.

Abram knew that his father was dead. Yet his father could not be dead. This could not be.

A gap in time began when Abram saw the back of that blue shirt in the lamplight and knew what he refused to know. He plunged down into the well with a coil of rope, looped it under father's arms and climbed back up out of the well, all seemingly in one swift motion. He did it, he did it numb. He must have done it, but he couldn't remember doing it.

He couldn't pull his father up hand-over-hand; he was just too heavy. The only way he was able to make any progress was to squat about a foot from the edge of the hole and take the line in his hands. He straightened his arms, leaned into the weight with his back straight and strained with his legs. Abram's stomach turned when, on his second heave, his father's heels dragged against the bottom of the hole as he pulled the body upright.

His hands couldn't hold the line, so he slipped them through the loops he had made earlier for the bucket. Then he balled both hands into fists so they wouldn't slide out of the loops and he pulled harder. Heave. Each heave brought his father another sixteen inches closer to him. Heave again.

Abram had to get him out of that well. Another heave. He would get his father out of that hole. Heave against the weight. He was bringing him up out of that hole. Heave against the sorrowful times to come.

When the edge of the pit crumbled and Abram lost a couple of feet, it was more than he could take. He knew he was going to drop his father. He knew that he would now have to dig the next well alone. He would now have to do everything alone. He sat stuck, unable to lift anymore yet unwilling to let go.

A cry rose within him. Why not just curl up and quit? Just let go and run for his mother? She would send for help. The cry uncovered and laid bare before him the choice that was his alone to make. No one would blame him. No one could expect him to do it himself. Abram rebelled. No, there was no help to send for. No, he would not quit and let someone else do his job. Yes, he could do this. Abram heaved.

His father's body appeared. With the last heave, Abram pulled him up and out. He cradled his father's head to stop it from hitting the ground too hard. Why? He wondered at that. He collapsed kneeling next to his father.

Abram didn't question what to do next. He threw the line and the bucket into the well and went down after them. Digging now wasn't as easy as it had been before. By himself he filled the bucket, climbed up, pulled the bucket after him. Again and again, he climbed up and down with the bucket. After uncounted bucketfuls, the dirt beneath his feet crumbled and Abram sank to his knees in cold water.

The well was finished. He had done it. They would have water now. The well that had killed his father would keep them alive.

He spent a long moment alone there by the well. He would have to tell his mother and sisters that father was dead. There was a well to finish with a cover, a winch, and a pail. Father was dead. There was cotton to bring in. Father was dead. There were hogs to tend and butcher. Father was dead, and there was hay to bring in. Father was dead. There was milking to be done. He stood up and took one step towards the house. Left foot, right foot.

MOONLIGHT - OLGA HEBERT

a moon is the beating heart of night
a blue moon in August, obvious time to camp

chairs set near enough to the fire
we feel its warmth
close enough to the shore
we have clear view of fading sky

waiting, we place a minor bet
where on the mountain ridge
will the full moon appear
I lose so make the trip

to the cooler for a bottle of wine
we sip as we gaze at the moon
and each other in its light

earlier we'd been visited by a duck
seven ducklings trailing behind
"Shh. Don't move," I said
thinking we might scare them away

we laughed — realized they came

to demand duck treats
didn't we know the drill

a paddle to the far end
of the reservoir where we spied
an old snapping turtle, a tiny
webbed foot falling from its mouth

the mother duck returned, only
six little ducklings in tow
we gave them bread crumbs

I did not know then how well
how soon I would learn
to accept death

the moon returns to the night
my heart beats on

STORM - LEIGH GAVIN HARDER

skies cracked open
winds roared furious
the storm came surprisingly fast

all the bridges are broken
splintered telephone poles
rusted underbellies ripped apart

structures supporting two ton trucks
now twisted in deformed faces
scowling and gap-toothed

all the bridges are broken
trusses ripped, torn beams
no one can go anywhere now

not back from where they came
not to imagined harbors or villages
where the cottages are lined up side by side
curtained windows in gingham and lace
not to where they wanted to go
hoped to go
someplace distant

a future place

all the bridges are broken
roofs busted open
mailboxes blown away
black leather shoes buffed and shined
a red stiletto, strappy and lean
baby shoes tied together
broken bridges

Broken
and I don't know how to go
where to go
next

ROUTINE - JEREMY VOID

morning:

i wake up. i have no idea what time it is. there's no clock in our bedroom, i dont have a phone.

she is not in bed. i must have kept her awake all night w/my incessant snoring.

i lie there for a few moments, trying to conjure the strength to rise. it takes a moment and i'm up.

i lumber down the stairs. the glowing numbers above the oven say it's 6a.m.

she is asleep on the japanese mattress in our living room. good thing we got this mattress, cuz otherwise she'd have lied on the couch all night long trying so hard to sleep, but remaining awake, and in the morning cranky that i had kept her up all night w/my snoring.

i tiptoe thru the kitchen, trying not to wake her. open the door and go outside and light my cigarette and stand in the shade smoking it.

grogginess makes it hard to stand up straight. i lean and sway in the slight breeze.

in bed:

i lie in bed drinking a monster and trying to summon the energy to work on my computer. i stare at the screen but i cant get my fingers to move. finally it comes to me.
i sip my monster and type.
the dog looks at me. i can tell she wants to go out for a walk.

downstairs:

i carry the dog down the stairs and put on her harness. release her from my grasp.
she scurries over to the japanese mattress and sets her front paws on my wife.
my wife turns over and grimaces. the dog takes the hint.
instead she curls up at my wife's feet.

walking the dog:

she lets off a soft bark. a dog and its owner are coming toward us.
i cross the street to avoid a skirmish.
she starts crying. barking. i say: "c'mon, now. let's go."
i yank the leash and my dog yanks back. i'm stronger and i manage to maintain control.
the old man and his dog start crossing the street to meet me.
what the fuck is he thinking?
"he just wants to say hi," says the old man.
i grimace. spit: "she's not friendly w/other dogs."
he must be from out of town. the locals know this already. damn out-of-towners who now mingle becuz they plan to stay.

now that vermont has the least amount of covid-19 cases in the country.

back in bed:

downstairs i hear a high-pitched chirping. i look at my computer and it is 9:00. my wife shouts: "jeremy, it's time to get up."
"i'm already up."
i go downstairs and offer to make her coffee.

DRESSED - ROGER WATTERS

Bending over
to put socks
on is now
a difficulty
too obvious
to hide.
It's good there
isn't a clock
keeping track
of the progress,
or lack thereof.
It feels like
you've actually
accomplished
something
and need
a break
just because you
got dressed.

DINING IN JAPANESE - DEBORAH GARCIA

My mother-in-law's hands
are delicate and soft
from hot mochi cakes
nimbly rolled in pink rice-papery palms,
where silky gluten pillows
gently patted,
sift their starchy clouds into her sencha cup,
as if six-thousand miles away
Fuji is erupting
and tiny fragments of fiery relics
are carried on currents of ancestral plumes,
as though drifting through the vagaries
of a grandson's lips.
My mother-in-law's hands,
once used to stitch intricate Temari balls
bursting like kaleidoscope spheres in your hands,
Unfurl tremoring finger tips,
numbed from pressing balls
of steaming gohan grains
onto sheets of brackish algae
cinched to form little purses of onigiri,

washing the Sea of Japan
over your tongue.
When my mother-in-law's hands
pivot bamboo sticks between thumb and forefinger,
twisting steamy grey ropes of
soba, binding them together
with the exquisite fastening of the obi sash
knotted around her party kimono,
there are no flashy adornments,
only the soft hum of traditional hōgaku
through clenched lips,
where she is content to move
through the love containing us,
waving bamboo sticks in air
atomized in buckwheat and soy,
so that her scent is infused in your lungs
and your saliva pools into pockets of pearls
splashing boisterously into vaporous bowls of white miso.
My mother-in-law uses her hands
as if foremothers never died,
as if a distant mountain
is still
erupting.

DIGGING UP THE BONES –
NANCY HAYES KILGORE

Sunshine through a canopy of yellow, orange and red makes the whole world bright as my husband Jess and I walk the dog. The September air is clear and crisp, and, despite the fact that we are living in a pandemic, today feels like all of nature is uniting in a sense of wellbeing.

Our neighborhood, the Old North End in Burlington, Vermont, is a medley of two-story houses on tree-lined streets. Most of the houses were built in the forties or fifties by working-class families, although some, like ours, date from Victorian times when this area was settled by European Jews. The neighborhood was even called Little Jerusalem. Now the people here comprise a mélange of black, white, African, Asian, students, and retirees like us–old and new Americans living in single-family or duplex homes.

As we turn the corner, we notice, behind one of the houses, a construction project.

Jess stops abruptly, and we both peer down the driveway.

"What's going on back there?" I wonder.

"I'll go see," he says, and he's off.

Jess, the retired architect, gets precedence when it comes to curiosity about construction projects. Not wanting to intrude more of us into whatever is going on, I stay on the sidewalk with Daisy, the dog.

Daisy and I wait. And wait. I crane my neck trying to see down the driveway. Jess is talking to someone in front of a yellow tape barrier.

Finally, with an amused smile, he comes back. "It's an archaeological dig!"

Oh sure. I laugh. We're both reading a mystery series about a forensic archaeologist, and this would be a typical Jess joke. But this neighborhood isn't my image of an archeological site. In this neighborhood houses are packed side by side and almost back to back.

No, really, he insists. It's an old burial ground.

Now we are both intrigued. A dig in our own neighborhood? Here's a mystery, like in the murder mystery books. What could they be excavating?

The next day we mask up and go back to the site. Heads poke up from a deep hole the size of a basement, where six or seven people in yellow hazmat vests are bending or kneeling over outlines in the sand . At the edge of the pit, a reporter with a video camera is interviewing someone, so we squeeze in to listen.

As her team below scrapes and sifts, a short woman in a smudged work shirt and jeans talks to the reporter. This is indeed an archaeological dig, says Kate Kenney. Kate is Project Historian in the University of Vermont Archeology program.

The owner of this house, she says, had been excavating behind it for an addition, but as the workers dug out the foundation, they came upon something unexpected–a coffin-sized wooden box. It turned out to be an actual coffin with a skeleton in it.

They halted the construction project and called in the police, thinking it was a crime scene. The police determined that the skeleton was not recent and called the UVM archaeologists.

The Old North End, in spite of its dense population, is usually pretty quiet. Two hundred years ago, it was even quieter. Then, none of these houses were here, and this area was a vast plain of empty fields. And some of those fields, as Kate explains, were used as burial grounds in the War of 1812.

A few blocks from where we are standing lies Battery Park, a tranquil little park with a playground and scenic walkways overlooking Lake Champlain. But during the War of 1812, Battery Park was the site of a military encampment. There were barracks, an armory, and a hospital, as well as canons and gunners posted on it. From that spot, high above the lake, the Americans could spy British ships coming down the lake from Canada. There were several significant battles, but the soldiers more often died from epidemics of flu or typhus than from battle wounds. They were buried in the surrounding fields.

This back yard where we now stand was one of those burial grounds.

We listen to Kate's account, and when the reporter leaves, she is happy to answer more questions from us. Kate is a fount of historical information, and I think I could write a book about Burlington just from her descriptions.

This particular site, she says, held eight graves, but two of them, her team found, contained empty coffins. Medical students, most likely from the Civil War era, would dig up the bodies for their studies, grave robbers in the cause of science.

Other burial sites are scattered throughout this area, she says, and the team has already excavated some of them.

As Kate talks, we watch the women (the team is all women today) in masks and neon yellow as they scratch and sift the sand with fine instruments. Archaeologists, scraping away layer by layer, a slow and precise task that takes time and patience.

The pit they stand in is about six feet deep, and we can see rows of coffin-sized holes in various levels of excavation. The ground level was lower then, says Kate, and over time it has accumulated layers.

The layers look like mostly sand, I remark.

They *are* mostly sand, she says. The sand came from the deltas that were created by glaciers. Most of Burlington, she says, was built on this deltoid land.

When I come back the next morning, I meet a tall easygoing man, John Krock, the director of the program, who also is happy to talk about the project.

I notice, I say, that the coffin spaces look like the shapes of mummy's tombs, elongated hexagons. John says that in the early 1800s, they made the coffins as narrow as possible, and in that hexagonal shape they were tailored to fit the bodies in order to save wood.

Now I see, emerging from one of the depressions, a leg bone.

When will you be able to see the whole skeleton? I ask John.

Probably by lunchtime, he says.

At noon I come back. And now I see, at the other end from the leg bone, a skull. But rather than the excitement I expected, I feel something entirely different. Suddenly our gripping mystery has taken a turn. This skull is turned to the side and the jawbone is wide open. I hold my heart. It looks like this man died in agony. His skull reminds me of the figure in Munsch's *The Scream.*

Though I remember that most people die with their mouths open and reason that this probably means that no one closed this man's mouth at time of death, I am struck by the concrete reality and the horror of death, right here in what is left of a person's head.

This was a real person, I realize, a young man who left home to fight for his country, to keep the British from reclaiming our land, who said goodbye to his parents, who suffered and died, and they never saw him again.

I take a moment of silence as I feel the grief for all of these people buried in fields around the city, fields that now consist of buildings or back yards over their graves. People unknown and forgotten.

What do you do with the skeletons? I ask John.

The bones will be reburied in a local cemetery, he says. There will be a mausoleum erected and a reburial ceremony to honor these war veterans.

Like the layers of the earth, history is a series of layers, each built on top of the last, each layer forming the base for the next.

The Old North End, Burlington's oldest neighborhood, was, for centuries, like much of Vermont, Abenaki territory. When Europeans arrived, they pushed out the native people and founded a settlement, and after the Revolution, the territory became American. In 1812 the British again fought the Americans over it.

New layers of history were laid in the latter 1800s when immigrants arrived from Eastern Europe, and this area became a thriving community of Ashkenazi Jews. Ruach Hamaqom, on Archibald Street, remains the oldest synagogue in Vermont.

As the Eastern Europeans assimilated and spread out into other areas of Burlington, the Old North End became a working-class neighborhood, and in the early 2000s, people from Vietnam, Nepal, Somalia, and many other countries began to settle here. Now we Old North Enders embody the proverbial American melting pot.

As I walk home, I smile at two giggling teenagers, Somali girls in beautiful wrap dresses colored bright turquoise and orange, with head scarves to match. At my house I greet my nextdoor neighbors, Lal and Muna from Nepal, who always welcome me with gracious smiles. Newcomers who bring windows into other cultures, new kinds of beauty and spice, into this Vermont town.

From the ice age to the present, whether in the soil or in the air or in our genetic makeup, we carry the layers of history within us. Here in Burlington, our layers include American soldiers buried here, the Abenakis, the Ashkenazim, as well as our individual and ethnic histories. They dwell beneath us and beside us and become a part of who we are.

FORM 4-B, TO BE ATTACHED TO APPLICATION MATERIALS, IN CONSIDERATION OF EMPLOYMENT (REVISED 10-2017) - JONAH MEYER

1. Please tell us how you first heard about the many wonderful employment opportunities available here at Fortune Express Enterprises?

wandering the savannahs, suddenly free from the trees and their endless branching i mumbled to myself many new syllables, forming them over and over in the mouth – like trying out for taste new delicacies at a
generous buffet.

over tens of millions of years, my gait changed, i became uptight & upright – with expanded vision across these grassy knolls, an ever-increasing brain-size & hands with wiggling fingers now free to manipulate my environment for any range of reason and circumstances: some innocent, some rather nefarious.

2. Okay, then.
How do you see yourself fitting in – and contributing to – the business culture here at Fortune E.E., LLC?

i am a swan.
weaving poems from the ether.i make love to you – and
you, to me.
i am a lute: the music is
overwhelming.

3. Please briefly describe your strongest attributes.

Can we not just be
Still? & silent? For a moment,
Nothing but
Stillness, silence.

4. Please describe a time you were faced with a challenge
in previous employment. How did you handle the situa-
tion? Would you have done anything differently, in hind-
sight?

Sight is a funny notion, yes?
Ditto smell & taste & touch &
All the Etceteras.
You, in your lovely 3-piece suit contain
Multitudes. Musique. Poesie.
How can you not know this?

5. Great!

When are you available to start?

Just imagine: the
Earth, she revolves around the
Sun, whilst simultaneously the

Moon, it is busy dancing in-
Orbit the Earth.

All this without bumping.
Without any crashes.

Every day.
Every year.
What, pray tell, could be more excruciatingly exhilarating?

AUTHOR BIOGRAPHIES

Elisabeth Blair is a poet, editor, and multidisciplinary artist. Her publications include two chapbooks, a full-length collection forthcoming in 2022, and poems in a variety of journals including *Feminist Studies*, *cream city review*, and *S/tick*. She's honored to be a poetry workshop leader for the Burlington Writers Workshop. www.elisabethblair.net

Mary D. Chaffee's latest fiction explores the nebulous landscape between reality and illusion, sanity and madness. In a former life she was a writer-for-hire, creating everything from advertising jingles and scholarly articles to reviews for the late, lamented *Village Voice* and an off-Broadway musical that actually ran *on* Broadway – just way uptown. Her first novel, honed in BWW workshops, is currently available on Amazon, and she is in the throes of imagining a sequel.

Ann Fisher lives and writes in the foothills of Vermont's Green Mountains. She is Fiction Editor for the Mud Season Review, based in Burlington. Her work has appeared in The Sonder Review, Heartwood Literary Magazine, MacQueen's Quinterly, The Green Mountain Club News, and elsewhere.

Kellie Fleury lives in Burlington, Vermont with a grouchy cat and far too many plants. She enjoys DIY projects, textile arts, reading and travel (which she misses dearly) and has been writing in the shadows for most of her life. She aspires to earn her MFA in Writing.

Deborah Garcia is a speech therapist from NY, living in VT. She's a member of The Burlington Writer's Workshop, the International Women's Writing Guild, the VOICES Center for Resilience, and Tuesday's Children. She's a trauma warrior seeking enlightenment. She's published in anthologies; *GLORY: A Nation's Spirit Defeats the Attack on America*, and *The Legacy Letters*, (Penguin, 2011). You can find her at dagslp@comcast.net and on her website at www.worldtradewidow.com.

Malisa Garlieb is a mother, teacher, healer, and metalsmith. She's poetry editor for *Mud Season Review*. Her poems have appeared in *Painted Bride Quarterly, Calyx, Tar River Poetry, Rust + Moth*, and elsewhere. *Handing Out Apples in Eden* is her first poetry collection, and there's a second manuscript in the works.

Leigh Gavin Harder has written poetry and made visual art for many decades. Her poetry is informed by the iterations of change experienced in the natural world . She is a past fellow of the VT Writing Project and has led numerous educational literacy trainings. Recent poetry has been featured in ZigZag Lit Mag and The Northfield News.

Olga Hebert is a retired special educator who now has time to write for pleasure. She is a member of BWW and Venice (FL) Poets. Her poem "Tender Moment" was published in *The Mountain Troubador.*

Ray Hudson attends the Middlebury Chapter of Burlington Writers Workshop, where he benefits from the careful reading and discussions of his and others work. His fiction and nonfiction focus on Alaska's Aleutian Islands. His poetry hovers somewhere else.

Ben Johnson grew up in Oklahoma, then studied Ancient Greek philosophy at Boston University. He spent many years as a college librarian and working in and around organized labor. Ben lives and writes in Barre, Vermont.

Nancy Hayes Kilgore's latest novel, *Bitter Magic* (2021, Sunbury Press) began with digging into the bones of family history. Winner of the Vermont Writers Prize and a ForeWord Reviews Book of the Year, Nancy is a graduate of the Radcliffe Writing Seminars and a pastoral psychotherapist. Website: nancykilgore.com

Karen Kish taught high school English for 25 years in Essex Junction, Vermont. She and her husband Sandy also spent 15 years teaching high school in Poland, Egypt, and Hungary. Currently retired, she now enjoys cross-country skiing, traveling, biking, tennis, and is writing a memoir about their international teaching adventures.

Tricia Knoll is a Vermont poet who, thanks to her family, has a stockpile of several hundred wonderful postcards ready to mail. Her new chapbook, *Checkered Mates*, is out from Kelsay Books in April 2021. Website: triciaknoll.com

Kristin LaFollette is a writer, artist, and photographer and is the author of the chapbook *Body Parts* (GFT Press, 2018). She is a professor at the University of Southern Indiana and serves as the Art Editor at *Mud Season Review*. You can visit her on Twitter at @k_lafollette03 or on her website at kristinlafollette.com.

Jonah Meyer has been penning poetry since he could first grasp a crayon. A freelance writer and editor, journalist, photographer, and librarian, Jonah's poetry has been published widely. In free time, he jams-out on guitar and enjoys watching old SNL episodes with his wife—and better 4/5ths—Jaymie.

Sharon Lopez Mooney, poet, is a retired Interfaith Chaplain. Now living in Mexico, has a second home in northern California; she received a California Arts Council Grant for a rural poetry series; co-published an arts anthology, produced poetry readings. Her poems are published in several journals, anthologies and international publications.

Peter Snow was an English and drama teacher, bartender, warehouse worker, goatherd, and psychiatric nurse. As a storyteller, he performed in diverse venues across the US and Europe, from tea shops to open fields. He is the author of *Recoveries*, *A Rosslyn Treasury* and *The Shifty Lad*.

Jeremy Void grew up in Boston, where he played in a punk rock band called Lethal Erection. He has written a number of books, from poetry to creative nonfiction. He currently lives in South Burlington, Vermont, with his wife Michelle.

Candelin Wahl is an emerging Vermont poet and songwriter whose work can be found in *Stonecoast Review, Scarlet Leaf Review, MockingHeart Review, Red Wolf Journal* and others. She's a consulting editor and former poetry editor for *Mud Season Review*, and an active member of Burlington Writers Workshop since 2015. Visit her at candelinwahl.com or Twitter @beachdreamvt.

Roger Watters started writing when he came back from Vietnam, mostly poetry. Fifty years later, writing still provides him with an outlet to record some of life's experiences through the eyes of his imagination.

ACKNOWLEDGMENTS

The Burlington Writers Workshop would like to thank our vibrant writers' community for infusing our organization with so much energy, talent, and creativity. Despite the challenges of the pandemic, we continue to advance our creative innovations in surprising and propitious ways. Many thanks to our dedicated workshop leaders who help us share and hone our craft and who have encouraged and inspired us in our literary pursuits. Thanks to our many volunteers who put in countless hours with the planning and implementation of all that Burlington Writers Workshop offers. Thanks to Peter Biello, founder of the Burlington Writers Workshop and this series. Most especially, thanks to Kristin LaFollette for our cover photo, and to all of the writers for sharing their vision and artistry with us.

www.ingramcontent.com/pod-product-compliance
Lightning Source LLC
Chambersburg PA
CBHW070913100726
47907CB00008B/2305